W9-BCM-687

# MIRACLE ™
## ON 34TH STREET

Adapted by Sherry St. Clair
Based on the 1947 Motion Picture Screenplay by
George Seaton and Story by Valentine Davies
Screenplay by George Seaton and John Hughes

SCHOLASTIC INC.
New York  Toronto  London  Auckland  Sydney

TWENTIETH CENTURY FOX PRESENTS A JOHN HUGHES PRODUCTION A LES MAYFIELD FILM "MIRACLE ON 34TH STREET" RICHARD ATTENBOROUGH ELIZABETH PERKINS DYLAN McDERMOTT J.T. WALSH JAMES REMAR WITH MARA WILSON AND ROBERT PROSKY MUSIC BY BRUCE BROUGHTON COSTUMES DESIGNED BY KATHY O'REAR EDITED BY RAJA GOSNELL PRODUCTION DESIGNER DOUG KRANER DIRECTOR OF PHOTOGRAPHY JULIO MACAT EXECUTIVE PRODUCERS WILLIAM RYAN AND WILLIAM S. BEASLEY BASED ON THE 1947 WRITTEN FOR THE SCREEN BY GEORGE SEATON AND STORY BY VALENTINE DAVIES SCREENPLAY BY GEORGE SEATON AND JOHN HUGHES PRODUCED BY JOHN HUGHES DIRECTED BY LES MAYFIELD ©1994 TWENTIETH CENTURY FOX

No part of this publication may be reproduced in whole or in part, or stored in a retrieval system, or transmitted in any form or by any means, electronic, mechanical, photocopying, recording, or otherwise, without written permission of the publisher. For information regarding permission, write to Scholastic Inc., 555 Broadway, New York, NY 10012

ISBN 0-590-22508-1

™ and Copyright © 1994 by Twentieth Century Fox Film Corporation. All rights reserved. Published by Scholastic Inc., by arrangement with Twentieth Century Fox Film Corporation, P.O. Box 900, Beverly Hills, CA 90213. MIRACLE ON 34TH STREET is a trademark of Twentieth Century Fox Film Corporation.

12 11 10 9 8 7 6 5 4 3 2 1                                            4 5 6 7 8 9/9 0/0

Designed by Madalina Stefan

Printed in the U.S.A                                            14
First Scholastic printing, December 1994

Christmas is a wondrous time in the city, with twinkling lights and "Silent Nights" and scent of peppermint in the air. It is a time when parents tell children stories of Santa Claus and elves and toy shops on the North Pole, a time when friends sing carols in the streets. A time of faith in things unseen.

But there was one woman in New York City who had lost her faith in childhood fantasies. From the day that Dorey Walker's husband left her and her daughter, she built a wall around her heart and stopped believing in fairy tales. She never told her daughter, Susan, bedtime stories of magical woods and dancing unicorns, or handsome princes who rescue beautiful maidens and live happily ever after. She taught Susan that all those things were myths and that wishes do not always come true.

Dorey worked for Cole's, the grand, old-fashioned department store on Thirty-four Street that sponsored the annual Thanksgiving Day parade. The parade brought joy and laugh to people all over the city, but the employees o Cole's had heavy hearts, for their store had fall on bad times and unless a miracle happened, Cole's would be bought out by a cold-hearted chain store owner who cared only about mone

In Central Park, where Dorey was frantically overseeing details for the parade, she was called to an emergency at the Santa Claus float. It was the most important float in the parade, so she hopped on a golf cart and raced down the street. She wove around pedestrians and security guards and flew past drill teams and marching bands.

On top of the reindeer sleigh sat a mysterious man with a white beard and rosy cheeks, dressed in a worn, but distinguished suit and topcoat. On his head he wore a fedora hat and he carried a fine wooden cane over his arm. In his hand he held the long, leather whip from the sleigh.

"It's in the wrist," the old man cheerfully called down to a fake Santa who glared up at him from the street.

The fake Santa was a pitiful sight. His false beard hung crooked on his face, and the stuffing under his belt looked lumpy. When no one was looking, he took a swig from a bottle hidden under his wrinkled costume.

"You throw it out," the old man explained, "then, with a flick of the wrist, you snap it back!" The whip whistled and cracked the air.

"You better give me my whip," said the fake Santa.

"You're intoxicated," the white-haired man said in disgust when he smelled Santa's breath. "You're a disgrace. Do you know how many children are watching you right now?"

"Gimme my whip," the fake Santa demanded and tried to grab it away.

But the old man would not give the whip back. He wagged his finger at the drunken Santa.

"When you put on that suit, you represent something that has great meaning and significance to people all over the world. Especially children. I won't tolerate public drunkenness." He yanked the bottle of liquor away. "You should be ashamed of yourself."

The fake Santa, whose real name was Tony, bumbled around as he climbed onto the
sleigh. But he got the whip tangled around his feet and knocked the sleigh and artificial reindeer
off the float and into the street.

Dorey Walker wanted to scream when she arrived at the float and saw the mess. She fired
the fake Santa on the spot and ran after the old man as he walked through Central Park. She
begged him to ride in the parade and to become the new Santa Claus for Cole's department
store.

"Millions of kids are watching here and on television. Would you do it? Be our Santa
Claus?" Dorey pleaded.

The old man agreed to be in the parade. But he insisted on wearing his own Santa Claus
suit while he worked in the department store.

The parade started at last. Giant balloon characters swayed in the breeze. Floats, marchir bands, drill teams, clowns, and mounted performers marched and twirled and pranced past the cheering crowds that lined the streets. No one had ever seen a better Santa. Every child though Santa winked just at him or her, and grown-ups recalled their happy childhood days when they heard the old man shout in his deep voice:

"Now, Dasher!  Now, Dancer!  Now, Prancer and Vixen! On, Comet! On, Cupid! On, Donder and Blitzen!"

High atop an exclusive apartment building, a man named Victor Lamberg watched the Thanksgiving Day parade, too. But his thin lips did not smile and his icy eyes did not twinkle when he saw the Santa float pass by. Lamberg was the owner of Shopper's Express, a chain of 500 stores across the nation. His main store stood on Thirty-fourth Street, across from Cole's. Lamberg's greedy heart envied Cole's. He wanted to see the grand old store fail so he could buy it out and close it down forever.

Susan Walker watched the parade, too. She stood at the window in the apartment of Bryan Bedford, a young lawyer who lived across the hall. The view was much better in Bryan's place, and besides, she loved doing things with him. Susan had known Bryan for two years and she thought he was wonderful and nice. She often dreamed what it would be like to have a father. She decided that Bryan Bedford would be perfect for the role, if only her mother would learn to like him.

More than anything in the world Susan wanted to have a whole family—a mother, a father, a baby brother—and live in a cozy cottage in the suburbs with flowers and a yard. She had seen a family and house just like that in a colorful Cole's advertisement. Susan loved the picture so much that she tore it out and kept it locked in a box in her bedroom.

But Susan was a practical little girl. Her mother had taught her not to believe in foolish fairy tales. Susan never played games of make-believe or put her tooth under her pillow or wished upon a falling star. She never lay awake on Christmas Eve listening for the jingle of sleigh bells in the sky or the tap of reindeer hooves on the roof. So Susan watched the giant balloons and marching bands and the Santa Claus float without much excitement. After all, she had seen the parade every year since she was a baby.

"You know how much it costs to make this parade?" she asked Bryan.

"A million?" he replied.

"One point six," Susan corrected him. "And it's probably a big mistake because some guy's going to buy Cole's and turn it into a junk store."

"I think you should ask Santa Claus to give Cole's an interest-free loan for Christmas," Bryan said with a wink. But Susan did not smile.

"Bryan. I know the secret," she said in a serious voice.

"What secret?"

"Santa Claus. I've known for a long time. He's not real."

"Says who?"

"My mom."

Bryan Bedford sighed in frustration. Sometimes he wished Susan's mother was not such [a] no-nonsense sort of woman, but he loved Dorey anyway and he loved Susan like his own daughte[r]. He knew it would take a miracle for Dorey Walker to marry him, but he had lots of faith that his wish would come true someday.

Sometimes Dorey liked Bryan. After all, he was very nice to Susan and he even helped cook the Thanksgiving Day turkey. But that was not enough to win Dorey's heart. She vowed she would never, ever let herself fall in love and get married again and take a chance on sufferi[ng] another broken heart.

The day after Thanksgiving was the busiest day of the year for stores across New York City. Employees scurried about and crowds pushed at the doors, waiting for them to open. Soon the streets would bustle with frenzied shoppers who grumbled and complained as they hurried from one store to the next. Soon there would be fake Santas on every corner and the magic of Christmas would fade away.

The mysterious white-bearded man from the parade brought his own Santa suit to Cole's that morning and put it on. From his shiny black leather boots, to his silver buttons, to his luxurious ermine collar, he was the perfect Saint Nick. He sat on the Santa throne in Cole's workshop display, surrounded by toys and elves and snow. He even called himself Kriss Kringle.

Every boy and girl felt magic in the air at Santa's workshop. From his snowy beard, his twinkly eyes, his rosy cheeks, and his round belly to his deep, cheerful laughter—never had anyon seen a Santa look and act so real. He greeted the children as if he knew each and every one.

"What do you want for Christmas?" he asked a little girl who eagerly sat on his knee.

"I want a Patty Pollywog Transmutable Baby Frog that swims and sings."

"Those are a lot of fun," Kriss said.

But the girl's mother leaned over and whispered into Kriss' ear.

"Those things are seventy bucks. My husband's on half pay. I can't afford it."

When Kriss Kringle heard the mother's words, he nodded in understanding, then did a strange thing. He told her that she could find the very same toy at half the price at the store across the street.

"It doesn't really matter who sells the toys as long as the children are happy," Kriss said.

"That's the spirit," the mother cried out, overjoyed at Santa's kindness.

And so it went all day long. If Cole's department store did not have the toy a child requested, Kriss Kringle told the parent where to find it.

Douglas Shellhammer, the general manager of Cole's on Thirty-fourth Street, wanted to pull his hair out when he heard what Kriss Kringle was doing. He twisted his hands and paced the floor. Whoever heard of sending a customer to a competitor's store? Santa should be telling the parents to buy another toy and he definitely should not mention a competitor's sale price. It was only Kriss Kringle's first day and already Shellhammer decided he would have to fire him.

But then the customers began to compliment Mr. Shellhammer. They loved what Santa was doing and vowed that they would always shop at Cole's. Mr. Shellhammer and Dorey Walker told the store owner, Mr. Cole, about what Santa was doing and suddenly it sounded li a wonderful idea. That very day Cole's started a new advertising campaign all over town.

"IF WE DON'T HAVE IT, WE'LL FIND IT FOR YOU!" all their advertisement signs and newspaper ads said. Soon Cole's was busier than ever. Parents loved the idea that a big sto put its customers above making money and soon Cole's motto became "The Store that Cares."

Victor Lamberg was furious. His Shopper's Express store was big and fancy. But it was cold and unfriendly. His Santa display area was empty, while Cole's was filled with eager customer Now more than ever he wanted to destroy Cole's, and he blamed Kriss Kringle for all his problems. Lamberg called in his assistants, Duff and Alberta. They had to find a way to get ri of that jolly Kriss Kringle.

Although Susan Walker did not believe in Santa Claus, she wanted to please Bryan Bedford, so she agreed to go with him to Santa's workshop at Cole's. She sat on the knee of Kriss Kringle, looked into his pleasant face, and asked his name.

"I have many names," he replied. "Kriss Kringle. Santa Claus. Father Christmas. Saint Nicholas. In Holland, I'm Sinterklaas. In Italy, I'm Befana. I have to speak many languages because I travel a lot." To demonstrate, Kriss spoke Russian and Swahili, but still Susan was not convinced he was real.

"My mother is director of Special Events for Cole's. I know how all this works. You're an employee of Cole's."

"That's true," Kriss said.

"But you're a very good Santa Claus," Susan admitted. She pulled his beard and discovere
that it was real. She examined the silver buttons, the ermine collar, and the golden thread that
bound the seams. She was impressed, but still she was not convinced there was such a person a
Santa Claus.

"What would you like me to bring you for Christmas?" Kriss asked.

"Nothing, thank you. My mother buys my gifts. If I don't want something too stupid o
dangerous or . . ."

Susan didn't finish her sentence because her mother walked up, her eyes flashing. Dorey
Walker was very angry at Bryan for bringing her daughter to see Santa Claus.

"I didn't see any harm," Bryan said with a shrug of his shoulders.

"There is harm," Dorey insisted. "I tell her there's no Santa Claus. You bring her down ere and she sees thousands of gullible kids and meets an actor, a very good actor, with a real eard and a beautiful suit, sitting smack dab in the middle of a child's fantasy world. Whom oes she believe? The Myth or the Mom?"

Bryan felt a stab of pain in his heart. Once again he had unintentionally made Dorey mad t him. He wondered if she would ever learn to love him as much as he loved her.

After work that day, Kriss Kringle walked to the Central Park Zoo to visit the pen where ome reindeer were kept.

"The reason I haven't been by to see you is, I'm working at Cole's," Kriss said as he took ome carrots from his pocket. "All I have to do is be myself. But more importantly, I guess, is at I'll be doing what I most need to do. Prove myself."

The reindeer licked his hands and chomped on the carrots, their black eyes shining with love.

"People don't have the faith they once had," Kriss said while stroking Comet's soft, thick coat. "If I can help restore some of that it will be well worth it."

Following Kriss Kringle into the park were Victor Lamberg's two assistants, Duff and Alberta. They asked Kriss to come to work for Shopper's Express and offered to pay him twice as much money. But Kriss said no.

Duff and Alberta gave Kriss a ride home in a luxurious limousine that belonged to their boss. They talked about how Santa is able to visit all the children of the world on Christmas Eve, and they talked about sleighs flying in the sky. Duff and Alberta dropped Kriss Kringle off at a very old, dilapidated nursing home for senior citizens.

"He's completely out of his mind," Alberta said after Kriss got out of the limousine and
walked inside.

"Imagine Cole's hiring a guy as nutty as that. It could become a problem for them," Duff
said with a wicked smile. Alberta agreed. If they could only prove that Kriss Kringle was insane,
they could destroy Cole's reputation.

As the days passed by and Christmas drew nearer, the word about Cole's generous policy
spread far and wide. Business boomed at Cole's and every child wanted to sit on the lap of the
Santa Claus who looked so real.

One day a girl who could not hear or speak sat on the knee of Kriss Kringle. Susan Walker
was watching from a distance as Kriss began communicating with the girl in sign language.
Susan's heart was touched with doubt. Maybe he was not just an ordinary old man after all.

That night, Susan tossed and turned. She didn't know who to believe, her mother or Kri Kringle, who seemed to be so nice. After all, he spoke every language and even knew how to sign.

"You're positive he's not the real Santa Claus?" Susan finally asked her mother, who was sipping coffee and working in the living room. "What if we're wrong?"

"Sweetheart, we're not wrong," Mrs. Walker said.

"All my friends believe in Santa Claus. How come I don't?"

"Because you know the truth and the truth is the most important thing in the world. Believing in myths and fantasies makes people unhappy."

Dorey looked at her daughter's troubled face a moment, then added, "If I'm wrong, I'll glad to admit it. Ask Mr. Kringle for something that you'd never ask me for. And if you don't get it on Christmas morning, you'll know, once and for all, the honest truth about Santa Claus

Susan smiled as she hurried off to bed. She knew exactly what she wanted for Christmas more than anything in the world.

The next day Dorey helped Kriss Kringle prepare for a TV appearance. The newspapers and TV stations and radios all wanted to do feature stories about Cole's new friendly policy, and they wanted to interview the man who had started it all—Kriss Kringle.

"You think I'm a fraud. You don't believe in me, do you?" Kriss asked Dorey as she adjusted his flannel cape. "Your daughter doesn't believe in me either."

"I don't think there's any harm in not believing in a make-believe figure."

"Oh, but there is," Kriss insisted. "I'm a symbol of the human ability to suppress the selfish, hateful tendencies that rule the better part of our lives. If you can't believe, if you can't accept anything on faith, then you are doomed to a life dominated by doubt." He paused. "You'll make a very good test case. You and your daughter. If I can make you believe, there's hope for me. If not, I'm finished."

As Christmas grew closer, Bryan Bedford's love for Dorey Walker grew stronger. He wanted to be alone with her for a while so he could propose marriage. One evening, Bryan aske Dorey to go out shopping and arranged to get a baby-sitter for Susan. But it wasn't an ordinary baby-sitter he had in mind—it was Kriss Kringle.

Susan liked having Kriss Kringle as a baby-sitter. All her friends at school would be impressed. Susan and Kriss had a wonderful time, but he couldn't believe that any six-year-old girl did not want a present from Santa.

"There has to be something you want for Christmas," he said that night as he tucked her into bed. "Something you want very much."

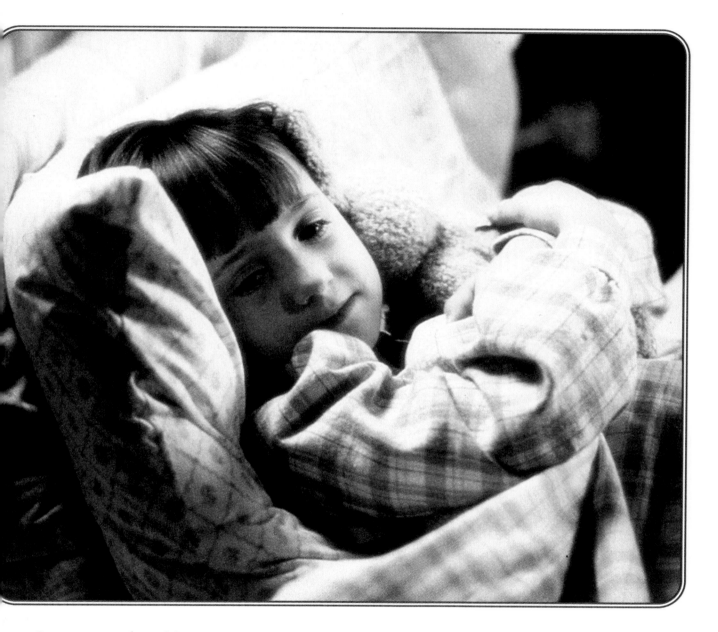

Susan remembered her mother's advice to ask him for something that she knew her mother
[co]uld never give her. But she was reluctant to share her special secret wishes. Cautiously, she
[ha]nded Kriss Kringle the photo that she had clipped from a Cole's advertisement. It was the
[pi]cture of the perfect family of her dreams standing outside a pretty suburban house.  Susan had
[loo]ked at the picture so many times that it was crinkled and worn. That was her Christmas
[wi]sh.

"If Santa Claus really could make reindeer fly and go up and down people's chimneys and
[m]ake millions of toys and go all around the world in one night, he could get somebody a house
[an]d a brother and a dad. Right?" Susan asked hopefully.

Kriss Kringle took the picture, but made no promises, for it was a very tall order, even for
[Sa]nta Claus.

That evening, while Kriss baby-sat with Susan, Dorey and Bryan shopped, then ate dinn
at a restaurant. All around them Christmas filled the air. Lights twinkled merrily on buildings
and in trees. The smell of Christmas trees and gingerbread and peppermint drifted on the
breeze. Even Dorey let down her guard and a smidgen of Christmas spirit sneaked into her hea
She smiled and laughed and relaxed for the first time in many months.

At the skating rink in Central Park, skaters began singing "O Come All Ye Faithful." U
and down the avenue people joined in—the mounted police officers, joggers, cabdrivers, old
men, and little children. Dorey felt so good, she opened her mouth and sang at the top of her
voice with Bryan.

Bryan's heart was filled with joy and love and hope as they returned to their apartment
building. This was the moment he had been waiting for. He gently removed a beautiful engagem
ring from his pocket and showed it to Dorey.

But Dorey did not say "yes" as he had hoped. She was shocked and angry and afraid of
_ling in love again. Instead of smiling and hugging each other, they began to argue.

"You've got a lot of nerve doing this to me," she shouted as she turned to go. Bryan loved
_r, but nothing he said would make Dorey change her mind.

"I've done everything I could to try and make you happy," Bryan said at last. "I love your
_ughter like she's my own. I've loved you, getting nothing in return, never asking anything in
_turn. I put my faith in you."

"You're a fool," Dorey replied.

"At least I'm not living a life of doubt," Bryan called out as Dorey ran away.

A wave of frustration and hopelessness swept over Bryan as he stood outside and watched Dorey hurry into her apartment building. In a moment Kriss Kringle came out. When Bryan told him about the fight, Kriss' cheerful face grew sad. Just before Kriss climbed into his cab, Bryan handed him Dorey's engagement ring.

"In your line of work, I'm sure you can find some lucky guy to give this to," Bryan said a sad voice. After two years, his faith was gone and he was giving up on winning Dorey Walk heart.

"I know what you want for Christmas," Kriss said as Bryan walked away. "I'll see what can do."

That very same night, Victor Lamberg's assistant, Duff, found Tony, the fake Santa who
ad been fired from Cole's at the Thanksgiving Day parade. Tony still hated Cole's department
ore for firing him and he especially hated Kriss Kringle for taking his place. Duff gave Tony a
isp one hundred dollar bill.

"I've got a little job for you," Duff said with a wicked smile.

The next day Tony showed up at Cole's looking for trouble. He flirted with Santa's helpers
d insulted Kriss Kringle in front of all the children.

"That guy up there ain't the real Santa Claus," Tony said with a sneer. "He don't live at
e North Pole. He lives in a nursing home on 114th Street. He's a fake."

Kriss Kringle was so mad he was ready to explode, but there were children all around
m, so he held back his temper.

That evening, on the way home from work, Kriss Kringle saw Tony waiting for him. Tony badgered Kriss and said terrible things about Santa Claus. This time Kriss lost his temp and swung his cane at Tony, but he missed. Tony fell to the ground and pretended to be hit anyw

From out of nowhere a photographer's camera flashed, and a police officer came runnin Duff and Alberta waited in a car nearby. They smiled as they watched Santa Claus being haul away by the policeman. Their boss, Mr. Lamberg, would be very pleased.

The news spread quickly that Cole's Santa Claus had been taken to Bellevue Hospital, place where insane people are put. A sadness descended over Cole's store, from the doorman t the clerks to Santa's helpers at the workshop display. Even Dorey Walker felt bad. She remembe Kriss Kringle's twinkling eyes and his kindness to children and his words to her:

"If you can't accept anything on faith, then you are doomed to a life dominated by doubt."

Suddenly Dorey knew that she could not forsake the kind, harmless old man and let him
to the insane asylum just because he claimed to be Santa Claus. She swallowed her pride and
lled Bryan Bedford and asked him to be Kriss Kringle's lawyer.

Deep inside the court building, in the judge's chambers, the city prosecutor, Ed Collins,
ed to talk the judge into signing papers that would have Kriss Kringle declared insane and
t away. After all, he argued, anyone who claimed to be Santa Claus must be crazy. And besides
at, the prosecutor's friend, Victor Lamberg, had promised to give the judge a lot of money for
s reelection campaign. The future of Kriss Kringle did not look very bright.

But suddenly the door opened and Bryan Bedford stepped in.

"If Your Honor pleases," he said. "I request a formal hearing to which I may bring witnesse[s]"

"Thursday morning. Nine o'clock," the judge grumbled.

Later that day Bryan visited Kriss Kringle in his room at Bellevue. The twinkle was g[one] from the old man's eyes and he barely managed a smile.

"I've disgraced myself," Kriss Kringle said softly.

"You defended your honor, you stood up for the dignity of every child. That isn't a disgr[ace] Kriss. That's decency."

After Bryan explained that the whole incident had been set up by Victor Lamberg's sp[ies,] Kriss straightened his shoulders and the twinkle returned to his eyes. He was ready to face hi[s] accusers and prove his sanity.

"I'm ready, counselor," he said with determination.

The story of Kriss Kringle's upcoming sanity hearing was splashed across the front pages of all the newspapers. The general manager of Cole's, Mr. Shellhammer, was terribly embarrassed that their Santa Claus might be committed, so he wrote a news release claiming that Cole's department store would have nothing to do with Kriss anymore.

When Dorey Walker read the news release, fire burned in her eyes. She stormed into Shellhammer's office and waved the sheet of paper in his face, then she marched into Mr. Cole's office and interrupted an important meeting.

"I just read your press release," she barked. "You're all a bunch of cowards. You don't deserve to run this store." She paused for a gulp of air. "We've spent millions telling people we're the store that cares. What about one of our own who needs us now? We credited him with saving the company and our jobs and our careers. That was yesterday. Today? We want to run from him and pretend we never knew him."

"What can I do?" Mr. Cole asked.

"If we stand with Kriss," Dorey said, "we'll save Christmas for Cole's and for everybod else. I may be thirty years old, but today I believe in Santa Claus."

Mr. Cole and the board of directors agreed with Dorey. Cole's quickly launched a televis commercial. Mr. Cole stood in front of Santa's workshop and defended the honor of Kriss Kringle.

"Cole's believes in Santa Claus," he said in the conclusion of his speech. "We will stand him. He has done nothing but serve the children and the families of New York City. And the world. We invite you to stand with us and ask yourself one simple question . . . do *you* believ Santa Claus?"

Suddenly the switchboard at Cole's lit up with calls from customers. All over New York
people stopped what they were doing to send a message. In Times Square the electronic board
flashed the message: "COCA-COLA BELIEVES." On a movie marquee the words read:
"GENERAL CINEMA BELIEVES." A gang member scrawled graffiti across a wall: "VICE
LORDS BELIEVE." And so it was all over the great city, from the rich and famous to the poorest
children in tenement houses, people scribbled their message: "WE BELIEVE IN SANTA CLAUS."

Thursday morning arrived. Newspaper reporters crowded into the courtroom to watch the sanity hearing for Kriss Kringle. The room grew quiet when the judge, in his flowing black robe, entered.

Mr. Collins, the prosecutor, stepped forward and called his first witness, Kriss Kringle himself.

"Mr. Kriss Kringle, do you believe that you are Santa Claus?"

"Yes," Kriss replied in a strong, firm voice.

"The State rests, Your Honor," Mr. Collins said and stepped away.

Bryan only called one witness, a little girl named Dorothy. She had received a dollhouse for Christmas last year and she pointed to Kriss Kringle as the man who brought it—Santa Claus.

"How can you be sure?" Bryan asked her.

"Because he looks like Santa Claus," Dorothy replied.

Prosecutor Collins leaped to his feet. "This testimony is ridiculous, irrelevant, and immaterial," shouted. "It hasn't been established that there is such a person as Santa Claus."

"Your Honor," Bryan said. "I would ask Mr. Collins if he can offer any proof that there is Santa Claus."

Judge Harper declared a recess until the next morning so that Prosecutor Collins could ther evidence to prove that there was no Santa Claus.

The next day the reporters and visitors gathered at the courtroom again. Everyone wanted see how Mr. Collins would prove there was no Santa Claus.

Mr. Collins' first witness was a college professor, a historian who explained how the original nta Claus came to be.

"Saint Nicholas was a fourth-century bishop in Asia Minor who was persecuted by a Roman emperor," he explained. "He was credited with a number of miracles dealing with saving children from tragedy. He was a recognized saint, but in 1969 his feast day was dropped from the church's calendar."

"In essence the church walked away from Saint Nicholas," Prosecutor Collins said and dismissed that witness.

Mr. Collins' next witness was an air force commander who had explored the North Pole for many years.

"Did you ever come across any evidence of dwellings, animal pens, barns, workshops?" Mr. Collins asked.

"No sir."

"In your opinion would it be possible for an individual to create a settlement in that inhospitable region large enough to manufacture at least one toy for each of the earth's one point seven billion children?"

"No sir."

Kriss Kringle suddenly leaped to his feet and shouted, "There isn't any way that the gentleman could have seen my workshops. They're invisible!"

"Kriss. Sit down, please." Bryan Bedford tugged at Kriss' sleeve, but Kriss continued to talk.

"My workshops don't exist in the physical world. They're in the dream world. I thought this was understood." Kriss sat down reluctantly as Mr. Collins called in his next witness.

The courtroom doors opened wide and two animal handlers led a beautiful reindeer into the room, its dark eyes shimmering in the overhead lights. The audience buzzed with excitement.

"This is a reindeer, Your Honor," Mr. Collins said. "I'd like the court to see if Mr. Kringle can make it fly."

Kriss Kringle rose to his feet.

"I'd love to oblige you, Mr. Collins, but I can't make the reindeer fly . . . they only fly on Christmas Eve."

"Of course," Mr. Collins mumbled, then turned to the judge. "The State of New York certainly has no interest in laying waste to a colorful myth but . . . Mr. Kringle is, regrettably, insane. It is my wish that he come under the supervision of the State so that the children of New York are not put at risk."

The courtroom bristled with angry cries. Kriss leaped to his feet; Susan Walker shouted, "Hey, you big jerk!" to Collins and pandemonium broke out.

"Order! Order!" Judge Harper called out and pounded his gavel.

Bryan Bedford stood when it was his time to call witnesses for the defense. He straightened his shoulders and stood tall in front of the judge.

"Your Honor, I have no further witnesses. I rest my case."

"I shall render my opinion on this matter at twelve o'clock noon, tomorrow," Judge Harper said.

The next day the newspapers blazed with protests. How dare the State waste taxpayers' money trying to prove there was no Santa Claus? Had the judge and the prosecutor gone crazy?

Cole's department store wanted to help Kriss Kringle, so the next day it took out a two page newspaper ad requesting people to show their support for Santa at noon, the same time as the judge's decision.

Victor Lamberg and his two assistants and Prosecutor Collins gathered in Judge Harper's chambers just before noon. Lamberg placed a briefcase filled with money on the judge's desk.

"The only way out is to declare this man insane," Lamberg insisted to the judge.

"My grandchildren think I'm a Scrooge," Judge Harper complained. "The bailiff gave me a dirty look. What about the people? What'll they think of me?"

"There's a hundred thousand dollars on your desk," Lamberg said angrily. "Does it really matter what they think?"

The judge glanced at his watch and saw that it was almost noon and time for him to announce his decision. Suddenly he heard a noise and rushed to the window. As far as his eyes could see, people on foot, in cars, in taxis, were cheering their support for Santa Claus. Traffic was stopped on the Brooklyn Bridge and people were jammed into Central Park and even around the Statue of Liberty. The unanimous roar of the people rocked the air and suddenly, as if by magic, the first snow of the winter began to fall to earth. Even Lamberg's assistant, Alberta, had come to believe in Santa Claus.

Judge Harper picked up a one hundred dollar bill from the briefcase and saw the words "IN GOD WE TRUST." Suddenly he slammed the briefcase shut and hurried out of the room. He knew exactly what he would say to all the people waiting for his decision in the courtroom.

At his bench in the courtroom, the judge held up a one hundred dollar bill for everyone to see.

"You will see the words IN GOD WE TRUST," he said. "If the federal government of the United States of America can issue its currency bearing a declaration of trust in God without demanding physical evidence of the existence or nonexistence of a Greater Being, then the State of New York can accept and acknowledge . . . that Santa Claus does exist and that he exists in the person of Kriss Kringle. Case dismissed."

A great cheer erupted in the courtroom. Bryan hugged Kriss Kringle and the bailiff shouted from the window to the masses below: "CASE DISMISSED! SANTA CLAUS WINS!"

Shouts rose from the streets. People danced in the fresh snow as it covered the dirty city streets with a layer of white as pure as an angel's wing.

Susan Walker watched her mother congratulate Bryan, but her heart sank when she saw them simply shake hands. It looked as if her Christmas wish would never come true now.

Bryan offered Kriss Kringle a ride home to the nursing home, forgetting that it was Christmas Eve.

"Home?" Kriss asked. "Oh, no, not tonight. I'm going to be very busy," Kriss winked, then said good-bye.

The newspapers spread the news quickly and everyone was happy, except for Victor Lamberg. Kriss Kringle's victory meant that Lamberg would not be able to buy Cole's department store. He stood in his cold apartment with bitterness in his heart, for in spite of everything, he still did not believe in Santa Claus and there was no magic in his soul.

That evening while going through her mail, Dorey Walker found a mysterious blue note written in beautiful handwriting, asking her to go to Saint Patrick's Cathedral after Midnight Mass that night. It was signed Bryan Bedford.

And on his office desk, Bryan Bedford found a blue note in the same mysterious handwriting requesting him to go to the cathedral after Midnight Mass. His note was signed Dorey Walker.

When Dorey and Bryan arrived at the cathedral, they were shocked to see a priest preparing for a wedding and to hear the wedding march booming in the background. But most miraculous of all, the priest was holding the wedding ring that Bryan had given to Kriss Kringle.

On Christmas morning, children all across the land opened their presents and squealed with joy. But Susan Walker did not laugh or shout or open the presents under her tree. The present she wanted most of all, a father, a baby brother, and a home, was something she would surely never have.

When Susan's mother stepped into the living room, a strange light danced up the Christmas tree and over the ornaments and across the ceiling and floor. Susan followed the light to its source. Suddenly her mouth flew open and her eyebrows shot up. The sparkling light was coming from her mother's new wedding ring.

"Holy smokes. . . !" Susan yelped.

Then Bryan Bedford came out of the kitchen and stood behind Dorey. With a shout of joy, Susan leaped to her feet and hugged the necks of her mother and her new father. The first part of her Christmas wish had come true!

That afternoon, after the pristine snow had covered the streets, and icicles dangled from trees like crystal chandeliers, Dorey, Bryan, and Susan rode in a taxi to the quiet suburbs outside the city.

"Mr. Shellhammer wants to take some photographs for next year's Christmas catalog," Dorey explained.

They stopped in front of the same beautiful house that Susan had clipped from the Cole's advertisement.

Mr. Shellhammer was waiting for them. He jangled the keys to the house in front of Dorey's face.

"You got a bonus," Mr. Shellhammer explained. "It's your house. You saved Cole's and we're all grateful."

"I knew it!" Susan whispered. Now, the second part of her Christmas wish had come true!

The air smelled clean, like fresh cut pine as Dorey, Bryan, and Susan walked arm in arm into the house. Inside, fragrant hickory logs burned in a cozy fireplace and warm, comfortable furniture greeted their eyes. Susan could not hold her joy back another minute.

"This is the house I asked Kriss for," she said. "He got it for me. And he got me a dad. And the third thing, I'll just have to wait for. But he'll get it for me, won't he?" Susan asked, turning to her parents. She thought how much fun she would have with a baby brother to play with and take care of.

"If Kriss said he'd get you something, I'll bet it's already on the way," Bryan assured her.

Susan bounced up the stairs to investigate her new room. But she paused long enough to lean over the railing and look down at her mom and new dad. The couple held each other tightly and their eyes were filled with love for each other and for Susan. A smile swept across Susan's face as she said:

"I guess there's no doubt about it. He's real."